AARDVARKS, DISEMBARK!

ANN JONAS

Greenwillow Books, New York

To my family

Printed in Hong Kong by
South China Printing
Company (1988) Ltd.
First Edition
10 9 8 7 6 5 4

Library of Congress
Cataloging-in-Publication Data

Jonas, Ann.
Aardvarks, disembark!/Ann Jonas.
p.   cm.
Summary: After the flood, Noah
calls out of the ark a variety of
little-known animals, many of
which are now endangered.
ISBN 0-688-07206-2.
ISBN 0-688-07207-0 (lib. bdg.)
1. Noah's ark—Juvenile literature.
2. Animals in the Bible—
Juvenile literature.
3. Rare animals—
Juvenile literature.
[1. Noah's ark.
2. Bible stories—O.T.
3. Rare animals.
4. Wildlife conservation.
5. Alphabet.]   I. Title.
BS658.J65   1990
222'.1109505—dc20   [E]
89-27225   CIP   AC

For forty days and forty nights it had rained steadily. Before the rain began, Noah had built a great ark. In it he put two of every kind of animal in the world and food for them and for his family.

Now the ark floated on water that covered the highest mountains. Noah and his wife waited. His three sons—Shem, Ham, and Japheth—and their wives waited. The animals waited.

On the morning of the forty-first day, the rain stopped. But they had to wait another six months before the flood waters began to recede. Finally the ark came to rest on the top of Mount Ararat. Still there was water as far as they could see. They waited.

Then Noah sent out a dove. When it returned with an olive leaf in its beak, Noah knew the distant valleys were dry. It was time to leave the ark.

Noah called, "Aardvarks, disembark! Adders, disembark! Albatrosses, disembark!" and continued calling the animals in alphabetical order. When he said, "Zebras, disembark!" he saw, to his dismay, that there were many animals still waiting in the ark.

Noah didn't know their names, so he could only call, "Disembark, everyone! Everyone, disembark!" When he was satisfied that all the animals were safely on their way, he hurried down the mountain to join his family. As he walked, he passed...

zebus

zerens

zorils

youyous

yaks

xerus

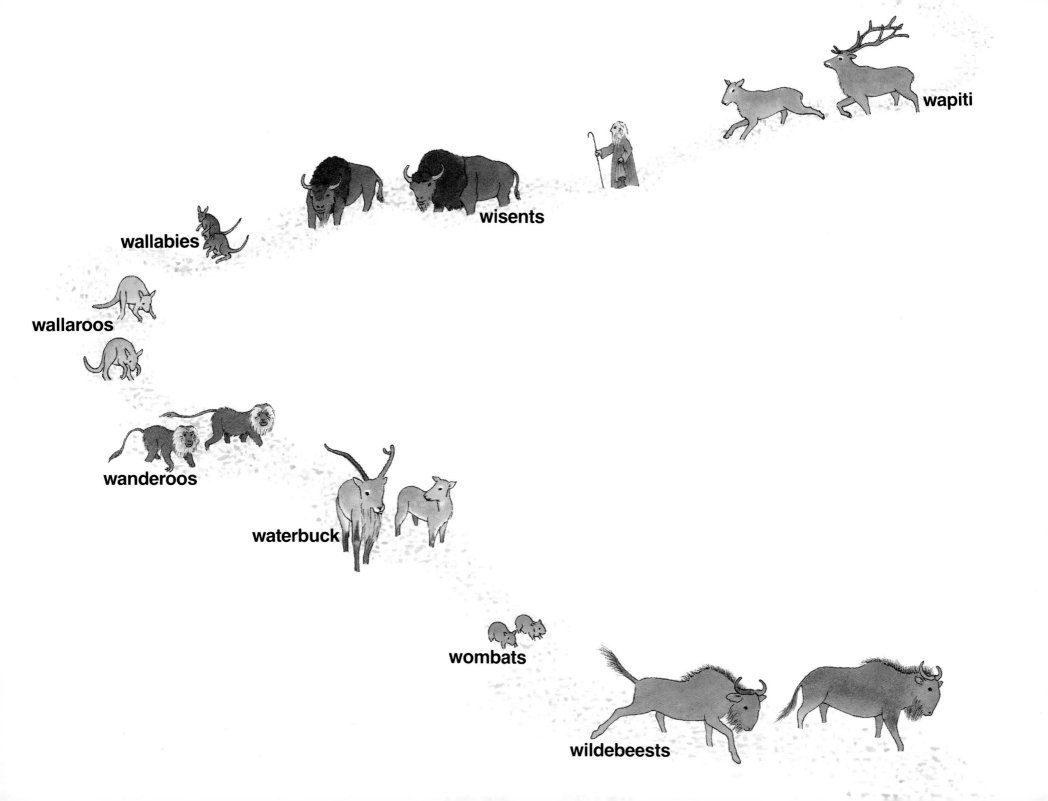

wapiti

wisents

wallabies

wallaroos

wanderoos

waterbuck

wombats

wildebeests

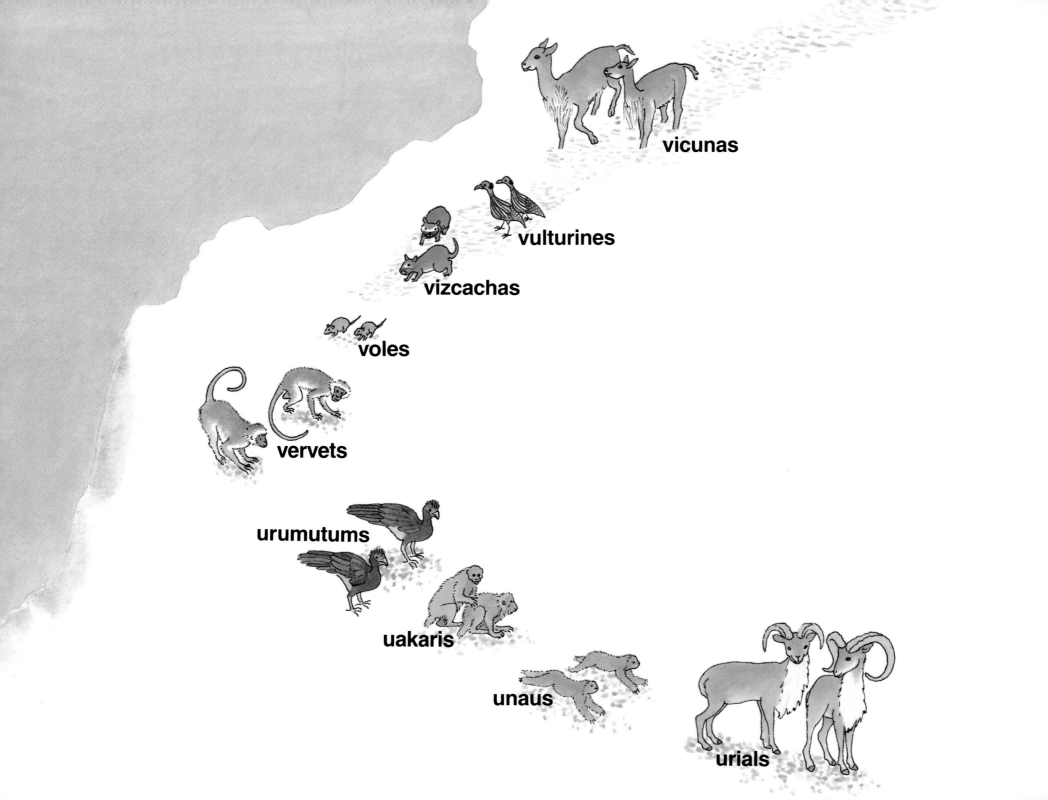

vicunas

vulturines

vizcachas

voles

vervets

urumutums

uakaris

unaus

urials

tahrs

tapir

tamarins

takins

tuataras

takahes

tamandua

tuco-tucos

thylacines

tarpans

servals

sikas

skuas

shoebill

saigas

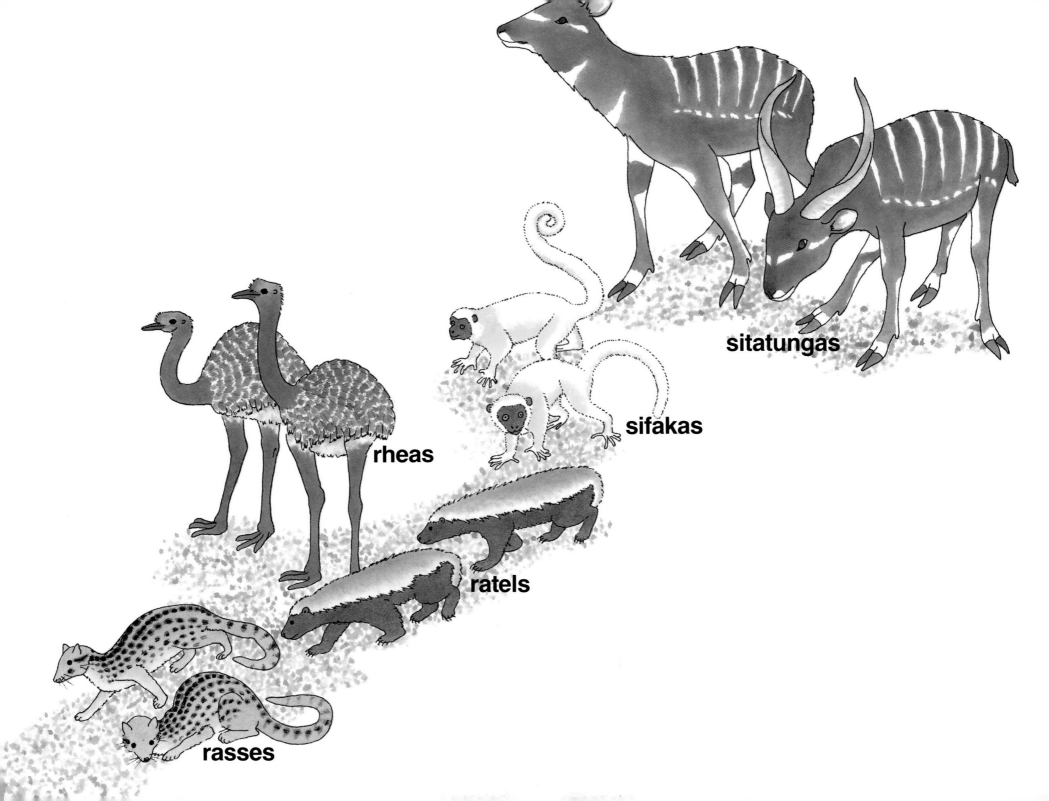

rheas

sifakas

sitatungas

ratels

rasses

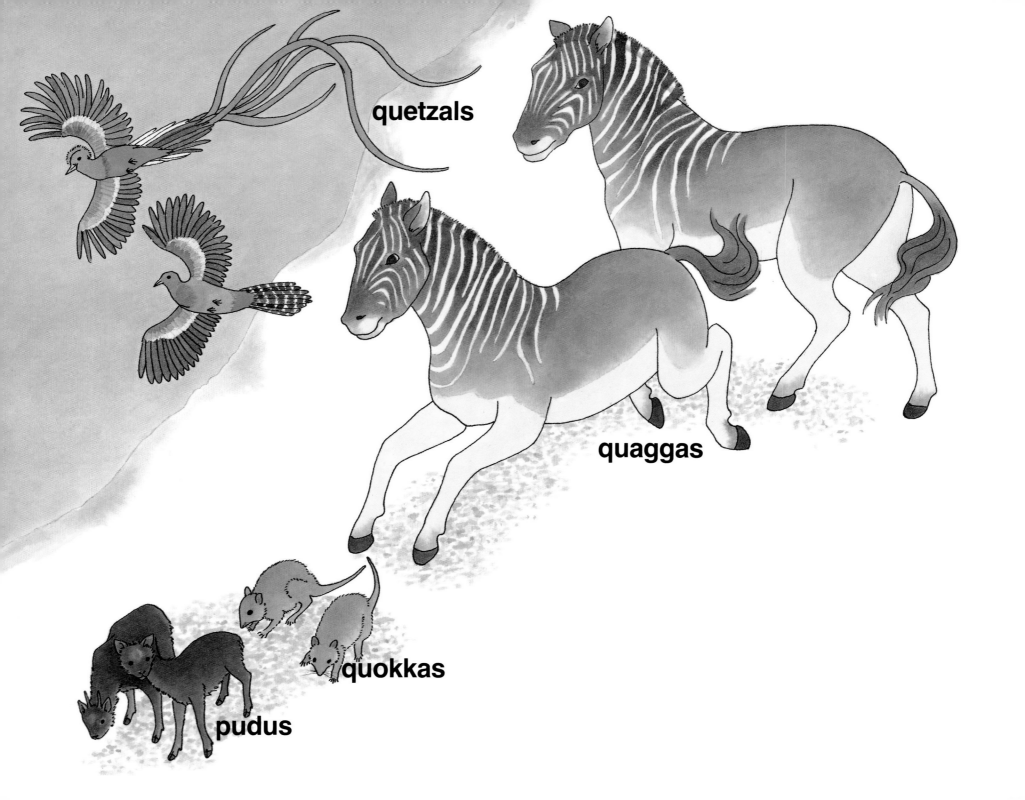

quetzals

quaggas

quokkas

pudus

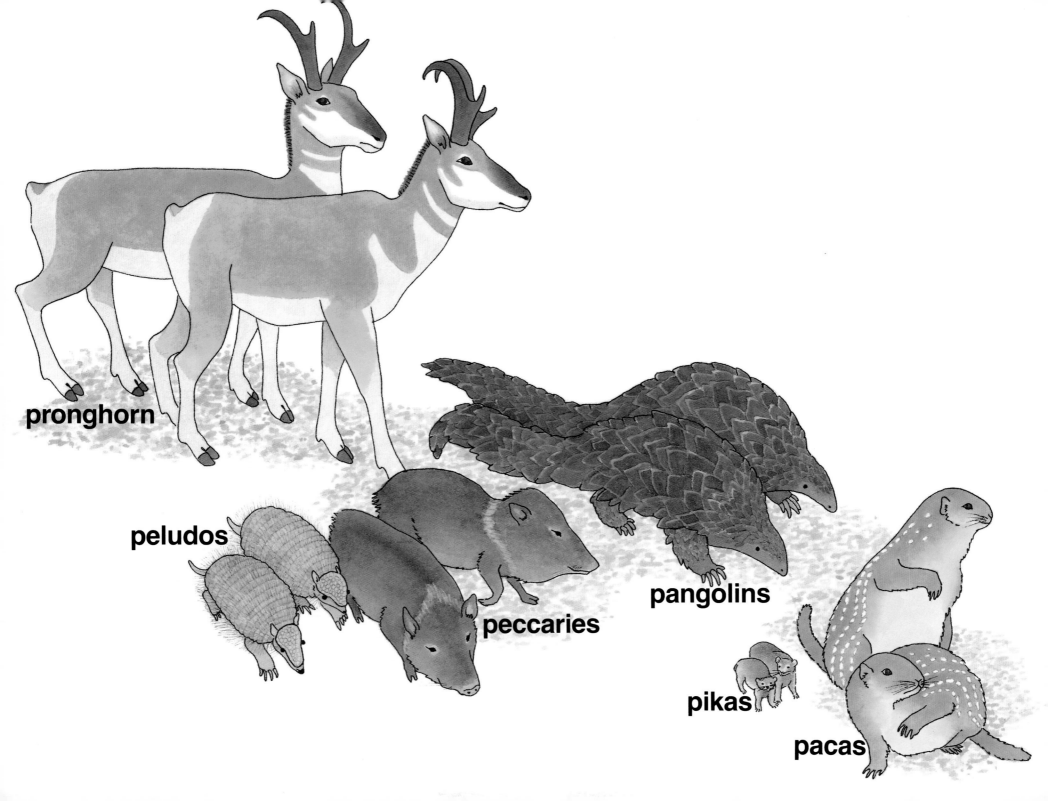

pronghorn

peludos

peccaries

pangolins

pikas

pacas

okapis

onagers

oryxes

ounces

oribis

nene

nilgais

nyalas

numbats

mee kats

marabous

margays

markhor

mouflon

lammergeiers

lemurs

lechwes

kiwis

kudus

kagus

kiangs

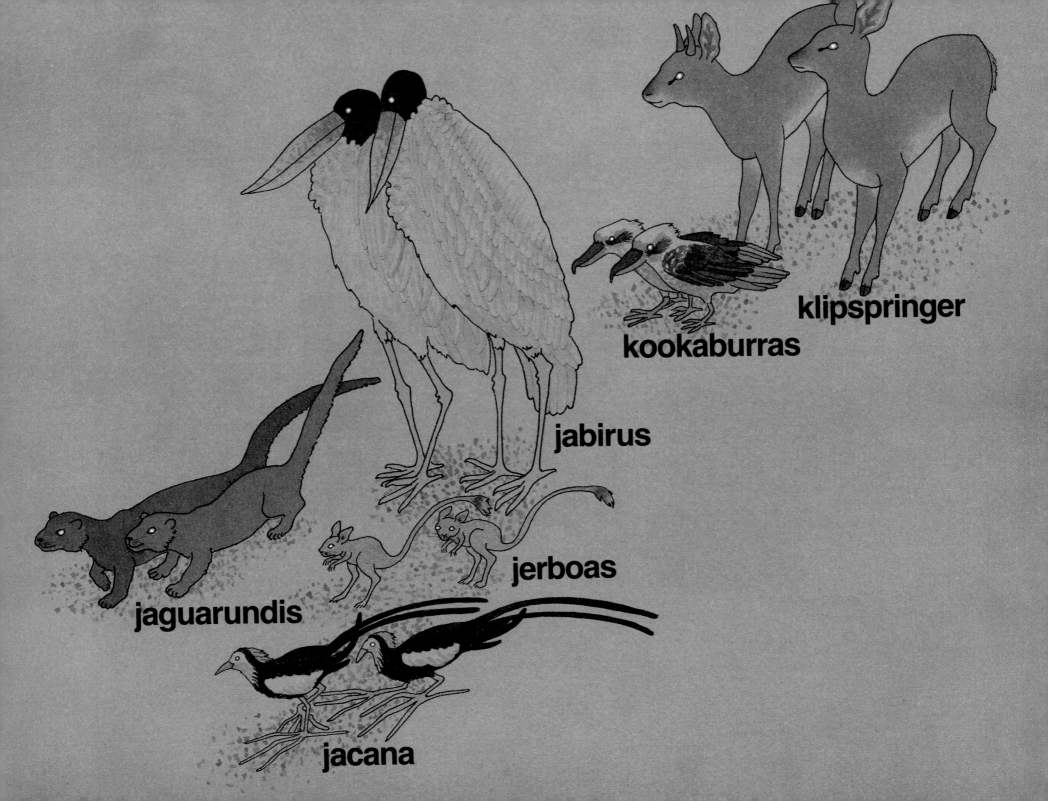

klipspringer

kookaburras

jabirus

jerboas

jaguarundis

jacana

ibis

ibex

indris

hammerkops

huanacos

hyraxes

hartebeests

hoopoes

gaur

gerenuks

guans

gluttons

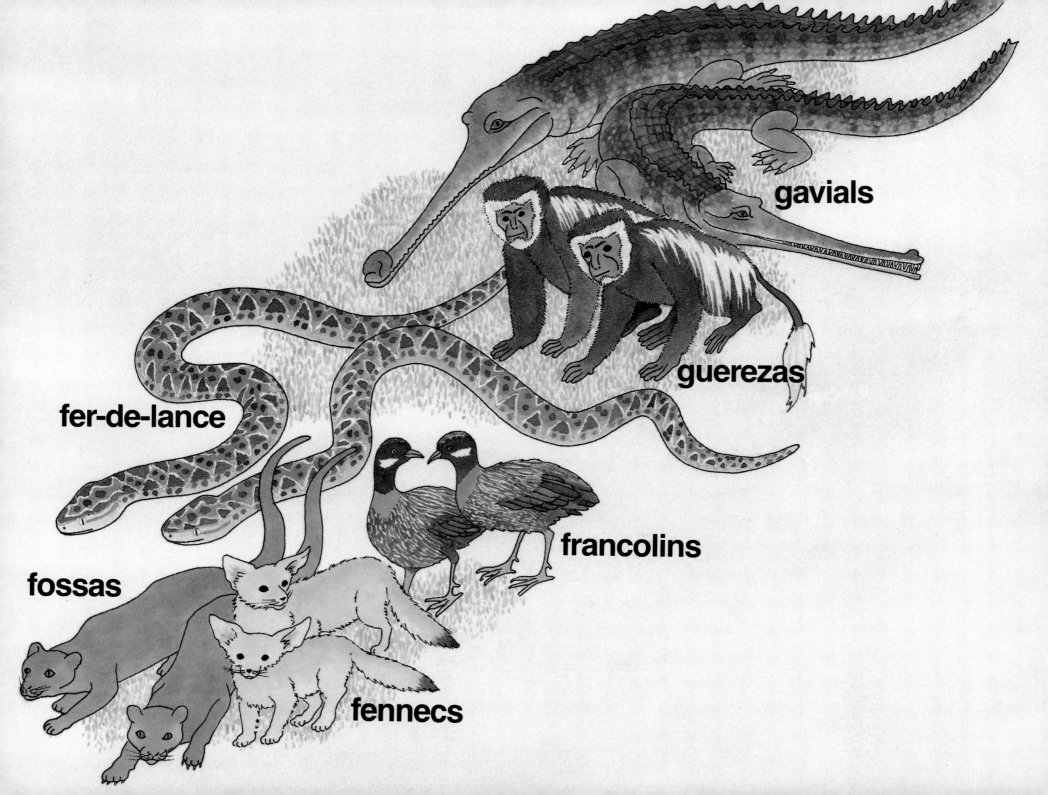

gavials

guerezas

fer-de-lance

francolins

fossas

fennecs

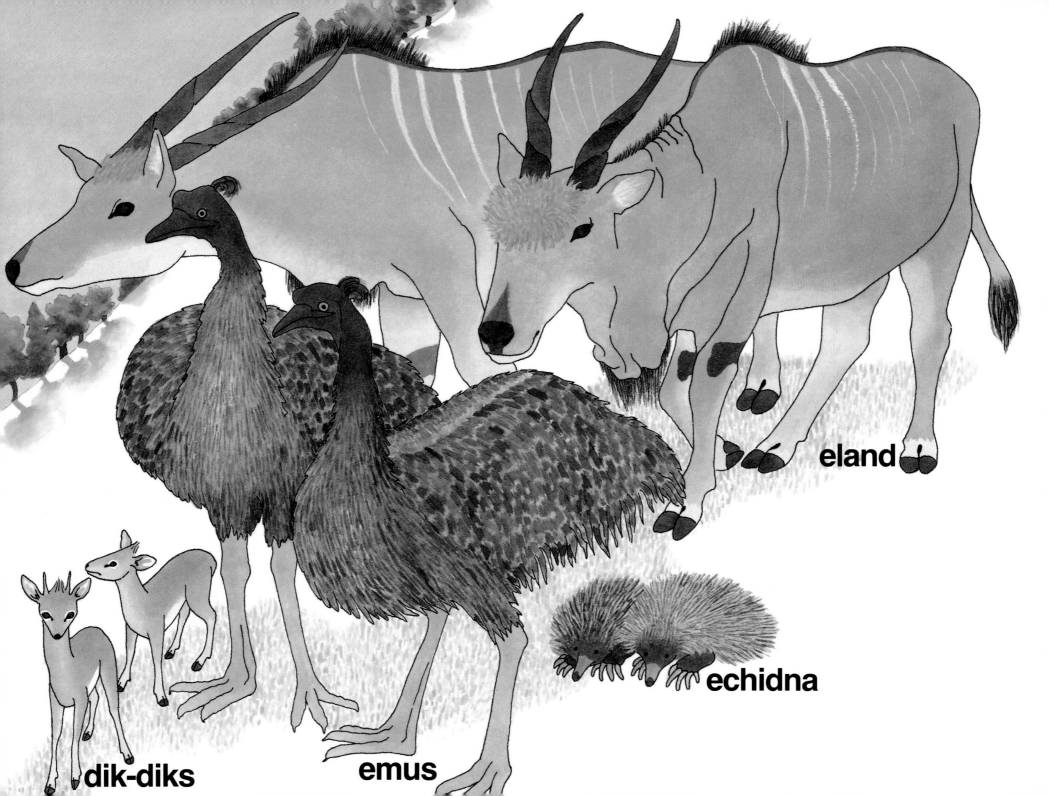

dik-diks

emus

eland

echidna

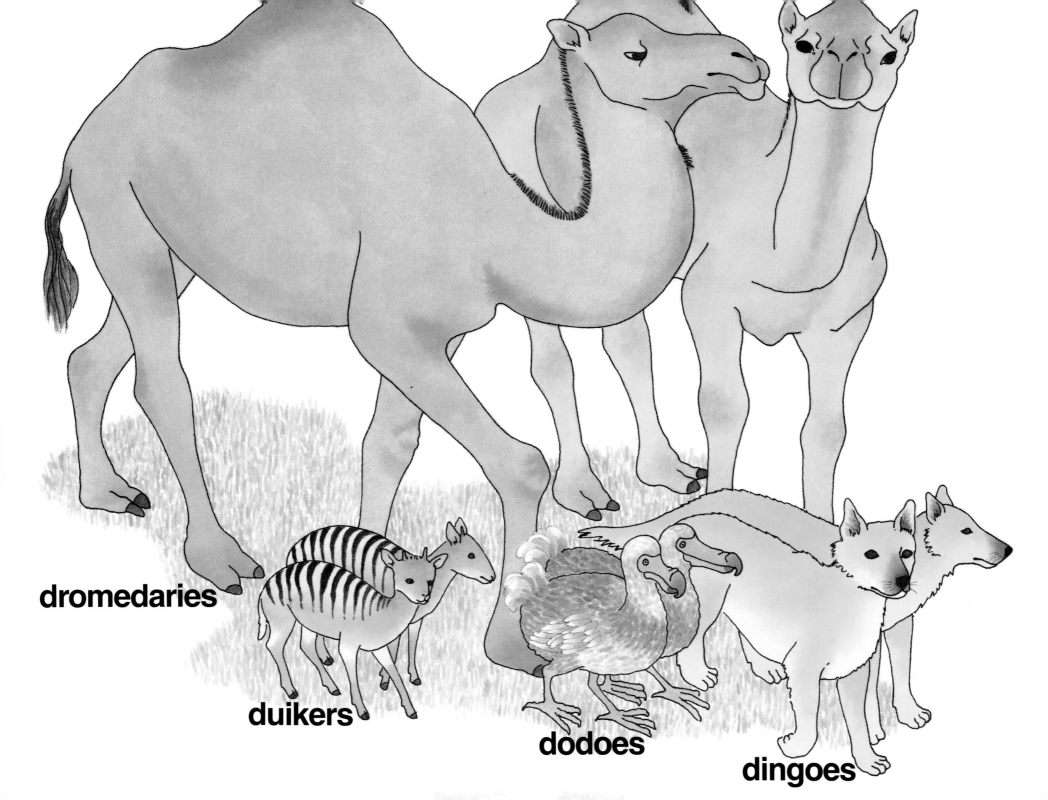

dromedaries

duikers

dodoes

dingoes

chital

cassowaries

caracals

cuscuses

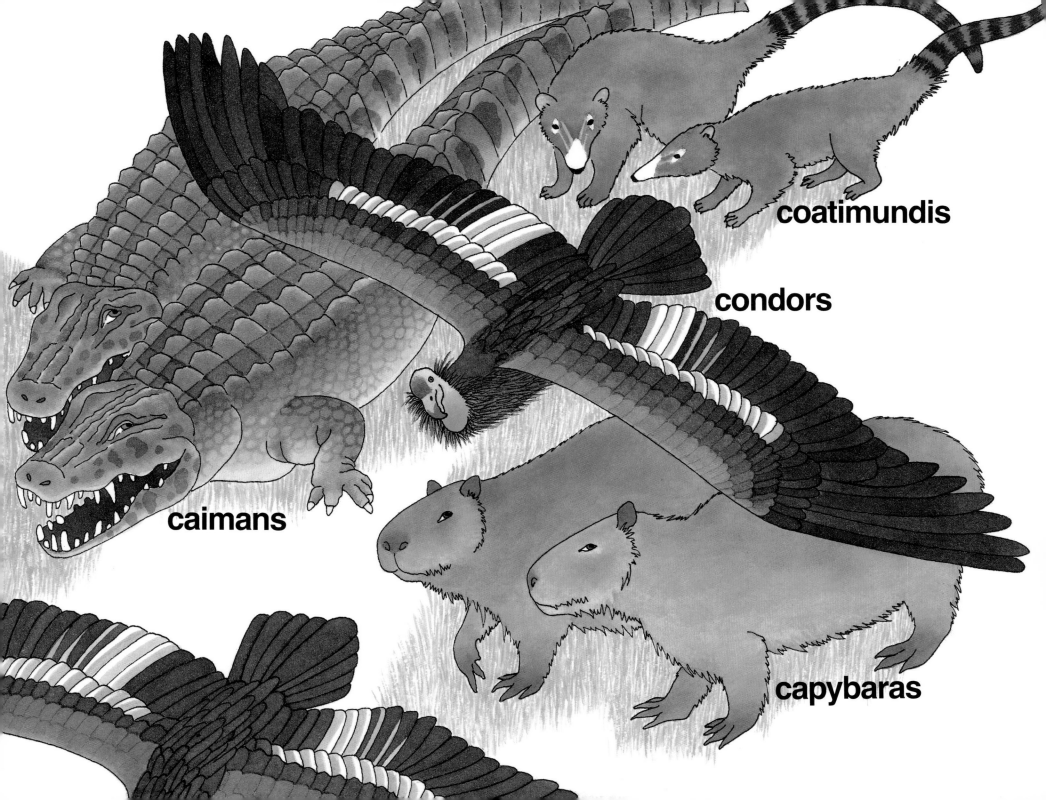

coatimundis

condors

caimans

capybaras

bulbuls

barasinghas

babirusas

basilisks

boomslangs

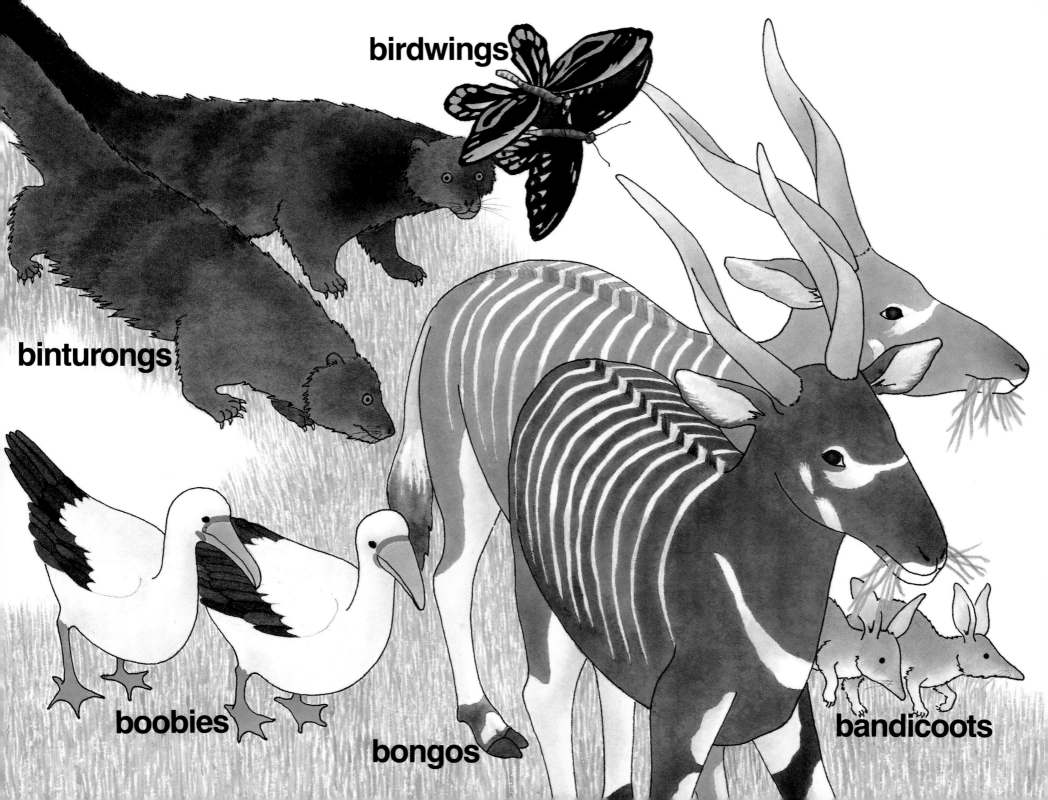

birdwings

binturongs

boobies

bongos

bandicoots

aurochs

agoutis

aardwolves

anacondas

aye-ayes

addaxes

anoas

and
aoudads.

Finally they all reached the bottom of the mountain: Noah and his wife, Shem, Ham, Japheth, and their wives, and all the animals from aardvarks to zebras and zorils to aardwolves. It was time to go home. Two by two the animals started on their way. As Noah watched them go, he called, "Take good care of yourselves. Take good care, everyone."

Then Noah and his family said good-bye to one another. Each couple went off to settle new lands in different parts of the world. And life began again.

Many animals that existed at the time of the story of Noah are now extinct. Many more are endangered. If we are to keep them from extinction, we must work to protect them.

One or more species of the animals marked with ● are endangered. Those marked with ○ are extinct.

aardwolf African mammal related to the hyena.
● **addax** Large African and Arabian antelope.
agouti (uh-GOO-tee) Rodent of tropical South and Central America.
anaconda Large constricting snake of South America.
● **anoa** (uh-NO-uh) Dwarf forest buffalo of Celebes.
● **aoudad** (OW-dad) North African wild sheep.
○ **aurochs** (OW-rocks) Wild African ox, extinct in 1627.
● **aye-aye** Nocturnal lemur of Madagascar.

● **babirusa** Wild hog of Indonesia and the Philippines.
● **bandicoot** Small marsupial mammal of Australia and New Guinea.
● **barasingha** (BAHR-uh-SING-uh) Swamp deer of India and Nepal.
basilisk Tropical American lizard.
● **binturong** Asian civet with a prehensile tail.
● **birdwing** Very large swallowtail butterfly of southeastern Asia.
bongo Forest antelope found in western Africa.
booby Small tropical sea bird.
boomslang Poisonous African tree snake.
bulbul Tropical songbird of Africa and Asia.

caiman (KAY-man) Central and South American crocodile.
capybara Giant South American rodent; relative of the guinea pig.
● **caracal** (KAR-uh-kal) Wildcat of Africa and Asia.
cassowary Large flightless bird of Australia and New Guinea.
chital (CHEET-ul) Deer of India and Ceylon, also called axis deer.
coatimundi (kuh-wah-ti-MUHN-dee) Mammal found in Central and South America; related to the raccoon.
● **condor** Very large vulture of California and the Andes.
cuscus (CUSS-cuss) Marsupial of New Guinea.

dik-dik Small antelope of eastern Africa.
dingo Australian wild dog.
○ **dodo** Large flightless bird of Mauritius, extinct in 1681.
dromedary Arabian single-humped camel.
● **duiker** (DIKE-uhr) Small African antelope.

● **echidna** (i-KID-nuh) Spiny anteater of Australia and New Guinea.
● **eland** (EE-land) Large, ox-like African antelope.
emu (EE-mew) Large flightless bird of Australia.

fennec Small, large-eared African fox.
fer-de-lance (FUR-duh-LANCE) Venomous pit viper of Central and South America.
● **fossa** Catlike civet of Madagascar.
● **francolin** Partridge of Africa and southern Asia.

● **gaur** (GOW-er) East Indian wild ox.
● **gavial** Indian slender-snouted crocodile.
gerenuk Long-necked antelope of eastern Africa.
glutton Large mammal of North America, Asia, and Scandinavia, also called wolverine.
guan (gwahn) Central American forest bird.
guereza (guh-RAISE-uh) Large African monkey.

hammerkop Large African wading bird.
● **hartebeest** Large antelope of Africa.
hoopoe Bird of Europe, Asia, and Africa.
huanaco (WAHN-uh-ko) Wild relative of the South American llama, also called guanaco.
hyrax Small mammal of Africa, Syria, and Arabia.

● **ibex** Mountain goat of Europe, Asia, and northern Africa.
● **ibis** Wading bird related to the heron.
● **indri** Tree-dwelling lemur of Madagascar.

jabiru Large tropical American stork.
jacana Long-toed wading bird, also called lily-trotter, found in the Americas and Asia.
● **jaguarundi** (jag-wuh-RUN-dee) South and Central American wildcat.
● **jerboa** Jumping rodent of northern Africa and Asia.

● **kagu** Flightless bird of New Caledonia.
● **kiang** (kee-ANG) Asian wild ass.
kiwi Flightless bird of New Zealand.
klipspringer Small antelope found in Africa.
kookaburra Australian kingfisher.
kudu Large African antelope.

● **lammergeier** (LAM-uhr-guy-uhr) Large vulture of Europe, Africa, and the Middle East.
● **lechwe** (LEECH-wee) Antelope of the African marshes.
● **lemur** (LEE-muhr) Nocturnal mammal of Madagascar.

marabou Large African stork, also called adjutant bird.
● **margay** Small American wild cat.
● **markhor** Large wild goat of Afghanistan and the Himalayas.
meerkat Mongoose of southern Africa.
● **mouflon** (MOO-fluhn) Sardinian and Corsican wild sheep.

● **nene** (NAY-nay) Nearly extinct Hawaiian goose.
● **nilgai** (NIL-guy) Large Indian antelope.
● **numbat** Australian anteater.
○ **nyala** Antelope of southern and eastern Africa.

● **okapi** (o-KAH-pee) Relative of the giraffe, discovered in Africa in 1900.
● **onager** (AHN-uh-juhr) Small Asian wild ass.
● **oribi** (OR-uh-bee) Small antelope of southern and eastern Africa.
oryx Large African antelope.
● **ounce** Asian wildcat, also called snow leopard.

paca (PAH-kuh) Central and South American rodent.
pangolin Asian and African scaly anteater.
● **peccary** Central American wild swine.
peludo South American hairy armadillo.
pika (PYE-kuh) Asian and North American relative of the rabbit.

● **pronghorn** Northwest American mammal resembling an antelope.
● **pudu** Small South American deer.

○ **quagga** (KWAG-uh) African wild ass related to the zebra, extinct in 1870's.
quetzal (ket-SAHL) Bird of tropical Central America.
quokka (KWAHK-uh) Miniature wallaby of Australia.

rasse (RASS-uh) Small Asian civet.
ratel (RAYT-uhl) African and Asian mammal resembling a badger.
● **rhea** South American flightless bird resembling an ostrich.

saiga (SYE-guh) Sheeplike antelope of northern Asia.
serval Small African wildcat.
shoebill Eastern African bird related to storks and herons.
● **sifaka** (suh-FAK-uh) Madagascaran lemur.
● **sika** (SEE-kuh) Small Asian deer.
● **sitatunga** Antelope of the African marshes.
skua Arctic sea bird related to the gull.

tahr Wild goat of the Himalayas.
● **takahe** (tuh-KYE) Flightless bird of New Zealand.
● **takin** (TUH-KEEN) Tibetan goat antelope.
● **tamandua** Central and South American anteater.
● **tamarin** South American marmoset.
● **tapir** (TAY-puhr) Hoofed mammal of tropical America, Sumatra, and Malaya.
○ **tarpan** European and Asian wild horse, extinct since 1876.
●○ **thylacine** (THY-luh-syne) Possibly extinct wolf-like marsupial of Tasmania; last known animal died in 1934.
tuatara Rare reptile of New Zealand.
tuco-tuco South American burrowing rodent.

uakari (wah-KAHR-ee) South American monkey.
unau (you-NAW) Brazilian two-toed sloth.
● **urial** (OO-ree-uhl) Asian wild sheep.
● **urumutum** Central and South American fowl.

vervet Monkey of southern and eastern Africa.
● **vicuña** (vye-CUE-nuh) Wild relative of the llama, found in the Andes.
vizcacha (viz-KOTCH-uh) South American chinchilla.
vole Field mouse, found worldwide.
vulturine Large East African guinea fowl.

● **wallaby** Small Australian kangaroo.
wallaroo Stocky, medium-size Australian kangaroo.
wanderoo Macaque monkey of Southern India.
wapiti (WAH-puh-tee) North American elk.
● **waterbuck** Antelope of eastern Africa.
wildebeest (WILL-duh-beest) African gnu.
● **wisent** (VEE-zent) European bison.
● **wombat** Marsupial of Australia.

xerus (ZEE-rus) African ground squirrel.

● **yak** Tibetan wild and domesticated ox.
youyou West African parrot.

zebu (ZEE-biew) Domesticated Asian ox.
zeren Mongolian gazelle.
zoril African animal resembling a skunk.